4/10

Bubba

By

Dave and Pat Sargent

Illustrated by
Jane Lenoir

Ozark Publishing, Inc.
P.O. Box 228
Prairie Grove, AR 72753

Sargent, Dave, 1941-
  Bubba / by Dave and Pat Sargent ; illustrated by Jane
Lenoir. — Prairie Grove, AR : Ozark Publishing, ©2001.
  ix, 36 p. : col. ill. ; 23 cm. (Saddle-up series)

  "Speed is not everything"—Cover.
  SUMMARY: In 1871, accused of being too slow in
pulling a fire wagon to the Chicago barn set ablaze by
Mr. O'Leary's cow, a bay fire horse finds a way to redeem
himself. Includes factual information on bay horses.
  ISBN: 1-56763-599-7 (hc)
        1-56763-600-4 (pbk)

  1. Great Fire, Chicago, Ill., 1871—Juvenile fiction. [1.
Great Fire, Chicago, Ill., 1871—Fiction. 2. Horses—
Fiction. 3. Heroes—Fiction. 4. Fires—Illinois—Chicago—
Fiction.] I. Sargent, Pat, 1936- II. Lenoir, Jane, 1950- ill.
III. Title. IV. Series.

  PZ10.3. S243Bub 2001
  [E]—dc21   2001-002667

Printed in the United States of America

iv

Inspired by

watching beautiful bay horses graze in lush green fields.

Dedicated to

all horse lovers everywhere. Try to be strong and proud, like a bay.

Foreword

Bubba Bay is a fire horse. He was one of the horses pulling the fire wagon when the fire house received a call that Mrs. O'Leary's cow had kicked over the lantern and her barn was on fire. A big area of Chicago burned that day because the fire wagon could not get there fast enough. Bubba Bay was too slow! He could not keep up with his friend and partner, a big strawberry roan, even though, again and again, he felt the sting of the whip on his rump!

Contents

Bubba

If you would like to have the authors of the Saddle Up Series visit your school, free of charge, call 1-800-321-5671 or 1-800-960-3876.

One

The 1871 Fire Wagon

The city of Chicago was quiet as two firemen led a team of horses into the corral. Bubba Bay watched as they removed the bridles from his piebald and grullo friends and turned them loose. The piebald lay down on the ground and rolled for several seconds before standing up and shaking his body.

"That feels good," he muttered. "Now I'm ready to eat."

"Me, too," the grullo said. "It feels good to be out of the harness.

I'm really tired. It's been a long, hard day."

Hmmm, Bubba Bay thought. It's been a boring day for me. I hope the firemen choose me for night duty. "They're expecting a slow night," he said with a chuckle. "And I'm the perfect horse for a slow night!"

"You sure are," the strawberry roan agreed. "I think you are a nice friend, Bubba, but I would not want to be hitched to the fire wagon with you on a busy run. The whole place might burn down before we got there."

"That's a mean thing to say," Bubba snorted. He pawed the ground with one hoof before adding, "But true. Speed is not exactly my best trait."

The firemen leaned against the fence, quietly watching the horses.

"I don't expect too much action tonight," one man said. "Shall we harness Bubba?"

"May as well," the other man agreed. "It would certainly please the fire chief. He sure likes that bay, but I don't know why. He's too slow to be a good fire horse."

"If it will please the chief," the other fireman said, "then we better harness him up for sure. Besides, the slow-moving critter needs to earn his hay like the rest of them."

"Humph," Bubba Bay snorted. "I may be slow, but I am alert and very dependable."

He walked over to the men. They laughed and slipped a halter on him.

"I believe old Bubba is ready to go to work," the fireman said with a chuckle. "Okay, Bubba. Let's get you hitched to the fire wagon."

Bubba glanced back over his shoulder and watched the other fireman slip a halter on the strawberry roan.

"Good," Bubba said to the roan. "I was really hoping to get you for a partner."

Fifteen minutes later, the bay and strawberry roan were harnessed and hitched to the brand-new 1871 fire wagon.

"I love being a fire horse," Bubba said. "My daddy would be proud if he saw me now."

"You do look good, Bubba," the strawberry roan agreed. "But be ready to run if the alarm bell rings. We not only need to look good. We need to be fast and efficient."

Suddenly people in the distance began shouting, "Fire! Fire!"

Bubba's ears shot forward, and he strained against the wagon hitch to see who was shouting. Seconds later, firemen leaped on the wagon, and one of them began to ring the alarm bell.

"Where's the fire?" yelled the fire chief. "How did it start?"

"Straight down that street," a man sputtered as he pointed north. "It's a big one, Chief. The way I heard it, Mrs. O'Leary's cow kicked over the lantern and set her barn on fire. Get going!"

"We're on our way!" the chief replied. He turned to the driver and yelled, "Get these horses moving, Sam. It sounds like we have our work cut out for us." The reins that were held by the driver snapped against the rumps of the team, and the strawberry roan leaped forward. But Bubba moved much slower. The fire wagon jerked and slowly rolled down the street.

The driver again snapped the reins against Bubba Bay's rump. Moments later, the bay felt the sting from a whip.

"Hurry, Bubba! Get a move on!" the driver yelled.

"Yes, hurry!" the roan agreed. "People's lives depend on us getting the firemen to the fire. Faster, Bubba, faster!"

The bay tried with all his might to keep pace with the roan, but he was unable to travel that fast.

The driver again slapped the reins against the rumps of Bubba and the strawberry roan. And again the roan leaped forward, but not Bubba.

"Come on, Bubba!" he shouted. "Don't be slow now! Chicago is depending on us."

"I'm moving as fast as I can," Bubba cried. "And yelling at me doesn't help me one bit."

Two

The Rescue

The journey to the fire was long and painful for the bay horse. He had never tried so hard in his life to be fast, but the effort was hopeless. I'm ashamed of myself, he silently groaned. My legs just don't move as fast as the roan's. The fire chief is mad at me, and I know that I'm a real embarrassment to the Chicago firemen. If I get through this night, I'll find a new job. Maybe I can pull the wagon for the milkman. He doesn't have to hurry all of the time.

Surely I can be useful to someone. A big tear slid down his cheek and fell to the ground.

Twenty minutes later, the fire wagon was on the scene. Firemen quickly went to work, dousing the flames that were leaping high in the air.

"What took so long, Chief?" someone yelled. "You should have been here earlier. The whole city is burning down!"

The Chief glared at Bubba, and the bay horse hung his head in shame. Moments later, one of the men walked up to Bubba, unhitched him from the fire wagon, and turned him loose.

"Get out of here," the man growled. "You are a poor excuse for a fire horse. Go on! Git!"

Bubba Bay slowly walked away from the wagon.

"I'm real sorry, Bubba," the strawberry roan said softly. "The man should not have yelled at you. It's not your fault that you're slow."

"Thanks," Bubba Bay replied. "But he's telling the truth. I'm not a good fire horse. I'm not good for anything."

Bubba slowly turned and began walking past the burning buildings. He noticed the fire was growing larger and larger and more ferocious by the second. Flames shot from within the stores and houses. The burning wood crackled and popped, and a thick layer of dark smoke filled the air.

A sad Bubba Bay was slowly walking through the streets of the burning city, when suddenly, he heard a strange sound. He stopped and listened several seconds before hearing it again.

"Help! Will somebody please help us!"

The bay walked toward the voices, but he could not find the source of them. Finally he stopped and nickered as loud as he could. The loud nicker pierced through the burning night, and then Bubba again listened for the voices.

"Hey! Up here! Look up here!" a high-pitched voice screamed. "We're up here!"

This time Bubba Bay was able to pinpoint the building. He trotted toward it. Flames were shooting high in the air. Through the thick smoke, he saw the terrified faces of three small children. They were standing at a second-story window.

"I must save them," Bubba said as he hurried toward the burning building. "This time I must hurry. Their lives depend on it!"

A moment later, Bubba arrived at the front door, but it was shut. He glanced up at the little children and nodded his head. I'll find a way to get inside. I know I can do it.

"That old horse can't help us," one of the children cried. "Where are the firemen? Why don't they rescue us? Firemen are supposed to save little kids, aren't they?"

All three kids began to cry. They sobbed loud sobs and begged for someone to save them. Bubba felt that his heart was breaking as he watched the flames growing in intensity. Suddenly he was very angry at himself.

"There is nobody but me here," he groaned. "And I'm going to save those kids if it kills me."

He reared high on his hind legs and struck at the door with his front hooves. The wood splintered, but the door remained closed. Time and again the bay reared and hit the closed entrance. Finally it fell on the floor with a loud crash. Bubba Bay immediately ran inside. The smoke made it very difficult to find the stairs, but soon he was climbing slowly toward the second story of the building.

"Here!" the children screamed. "We're in the bedroom, but the door is locked. We can't get out!"

Bubba turned his rump toward a closed door and kicked as hard as he could. The door collapsed, but the children were not inside. Two more times, he attacked other doors, but it was still to no avail.

A burning rafter fell beside Bubba. He jumped over it and ran to another closed door.

"This better be the right one," he muttered. "The children and I are running out of time."

Bubba gathered his muscles, backed up with his rump toward the door, and kicked as hard as he could! As the door crashed to the floor, he saw three terrified little children stumbling toward him. He felt good! He felt better than he had felt in a long, long time.

Bubba nickered softly and knelt down, and the frightened kids threw their arms around him, then crawled on his back.

Seconds later, Bubba Bay was carefully stepping down the stairs when another rafter fell. It hit hard and embers scattered throughout the building.

"Hang on, kids," he muttered through clenched teeth. "We're almost to the front door."

The bay horse stumbled over the threshold. His big brown eyes were stinging from the pungent smoke, and tears were streaming down his face. The hair on his sleek body was singed from the flames, and all four hooves were sore from breaking down the doors in his numerous attempts to find the little children.

As Bubba stepped outside, the roof collapsed. The entire building was in flames.

Bubba quickly walked to the middle of the street and knelt down. The children slid from his back, and he slowly lay down on the ground.

Three

The Hero Fire Horse

"I think Bubba's waking up!" an excited voice exclaimed.

Bubba slowly opened his eyes. People with worried expressions on their faces were gathered all around him. Hmmm, I must be dreaming, he thought. Why are these folks staring at me? Why am I laying down in the middle of the street? This must be a dream.

Then, three little children knelt down beside him. They stroked his nose and talked softly to him.

"You saved our lives," a little boy said. "I didn't know horses could climb stairs!"

"You are my hero," a little girl murmured. "I love you, Bubba. I wish you could live with us."

The third child gently stroked his foretop and said, "Thank you, Bubba, for saving my life. You are a brave horse. I'll never forget you, Bubba. Never, ever."

The bay heard a familiar voice.

"You are one fine fire horse. I'm proud to be your friend, Bubba."

Bubba Bay lifted his head and looked over his shoulder. The strawberry roan was standing near him with a big smile on his face. And next to the fire horse, Bubba saw the fire chief gazing down at him with a worried look on his face.

"Are you going to be all right?" the fire chief asked quietly. "You better get healed because you have a big surprise waiting for you."

"A surprise? For me? Why?" Bubba asked as he slowly stood up. His poor head ached, and he felt the sting from several burns on his body. But loud cheers from the gathering crowd did a good job of taking his mind off his problems.

Bubba turned to the strawberry roan and quietly said, "I don't understand. Why is everyone cheering? I am no longer a fire horse. Tonight I proved that I'm too slow."

The roan chuckled and shook his head.

"You're wrong, Bubba. You're the best fire horse in the whole wide world. The rest of us were real busy trying to save the burning buildings, but you did the right thing, Bubba. You decided to save the lives of these three little children."

Bubba looked at the children. Again they hugged him tight and he nuzzled them with his nose.

"The rest of us are plain old fire horses, Bubba," the roan said. "You are a hero fire horse!"

"I was always told that a fast horse was better than a slow one. But," Bubba muttered, "if I had ran past that building, I would not have heard these children crying for help. Hmmmm, it looks like it took the Great Chicago Fire to prove that a slow fire horse can be a hero!"

Four

Bay Horse Facts

Bay describes horses with black points and with bodies that are some shade of red. *Bay* is a common color and can be divided into several shades. At one extreme the body color is nearly yellow, and at the other extreme it is mixed with black and the horse can resemble a brown, seal brown, or black. All bays have red in the coat. This gives the color a certain brilliance and sheen.

The most common bay is the *red bay* (cherry bay). The body is a clear shade of red with very little variation in intensity.

Mahogany bays are sometimes referred to as dark bay and result from black being mixed into the red body coat. On some mahogany bays, the mane and tail can fade to brown.

Blood bay is another shade of bay, but instead of being a mixture of red and black as in mahogany bays, the body color is a pure shade of dark purplish red with little or no black intermingled.

The lightest shade is *sandy bay* (also called honey bay or mealy bay). In the sandy bay the body is a light red that approaches yellow.

All horses are divided into two groups on the basis of the color of the point: .horses with black points and horses with nonblack points. The nonblack points span a spectrum from brown to red to cream. Horses are described by their coat colors and markings. No two horses are identical, and colors vary within a category. The bay can be light, bright, dappled, or dark. The term *bay* denotes a red body with black mane, tail, and lower legs. Although two colors are present (black and red), one horse color name is used to indicate the combination.

The various groups of horse colors with black points are *black* (body black), *brown* (body brown), *bay* (body red), *grullo* (body slate), and *buckskin* (body yellow).